FITTING ROOM TEMPTATION

GAY PUBLIC SEX SERIES #3

NICO FOX

CONTENTS

CHAPTER 1

JUST TWO YEARS out of college, I'd already upgraded my career with a 50% bump in pay with a new position in the Miami office. I needed to upgrade my wardrobe to dress the part for this new lucrative job.

But it's not just at work where I needed to dress better, my personal life needs a boost too. I'd done nothing but work to build up my career since leaving college that I've had no room for a love life, let alone casual sex. I'll need clothes for all occasions. Even when not at work, I need to dress sharp for casual events with coworkers.

When I was in college, all of my clothes came from the goodwill stores and Salvation Army. Five dollars for a pair of jeans was my limit, even if they had holes in them.

When I got my first job, I upgraded to the big box stores like Walmart. I'm not sure what clothes are fashionable these days, as I hadn't even been in a mall in many years. I'd only been wearing suits at work, sweatpants at home.

But you know what they say, you have to dress for the job you want, not the job you have.

I headed to one of the ritziest malls in Miami Beach. Outdoors, of course. People were decked out to the nines head to toe as they went to each designer shop.

These were stores that I've heard of, but never felt I could even enter. Gucci, Versace, Armani: these places weren't for people like me. Until now.

I found one of the less intimidating clothing stores. It was a smaller boutique store with only one employee. And a damn fine cute one at that. He stood behind the counter looking bored and engrossed on his phone.

He was too busy texting that he didn't even notice me walking. That was fine with me, because I gawked at him before he noticed. Those lips! Those goddamned juicy red lips I could swim in for days.

He wore a black see-through mesh shirt that showed off his swimmer's build. He had long arms and broad shoulders that created a V-shape on his back.

On the counter was a college biology textbook sitting next to a University of Miami book bag. After a moment, he scrutinized me and said, "Welcome to our store."

His lusty eyes signaled he found me attractive but at the same time laughing at my choice of clothing. My worn-out cargo shorts and a ratty old t-shirt were out of place in this lavish mall.

I nodded to him and browsed the store. There wasn't anything under a hundred dollars. I picked up a shirt with a feather-light fabric. It appeared it would flatter my torso, but didn't know where I could wear it.

"That shirt would look fabulous on you." I heard a voice from behind me. I turned around and the store clerk held out his hand. "My name is Sebastian. Let me know if you need any assistance."

He glanced at my outfit again and said, "Who am I kidding? Of course, you need assistance!" We both laughed.

"I'm Vince, I have a new job and need a wardrobe upgrade. I need to look my best at work and out on the town."

"Say no more." He took the shirt from my hand, turned around, and picked up three more shirts from the rack behind him. When he turned back around, I said, "I like your shirt," making it obvious that I was checking him out.

"I bet you'd look good in a thin t-shirt too." He grabbed one off the rack. "Try these on."

He showed me to the little hallway of fitting rooms around the corner, but before I went inside, his eyes ran the length of my body several times which made me tingle down below.

I didn't like the first two shirts I tried on, but I would definitely buy the dress shirt. Last, was the see-through shirt he gave me.

It was so silky smooth that it slid over me like butter. I loved the texture against my smooth chest. It even aroused me a little bit.

"Knock, knock," he said from outside the door. "How is that shirt working out for you?"

"I'll take it."

"Don't be shy. Let's see how sharp you look in it."

I opened the door and showed him the shirt. I felt naked as the shirt was so transparent. Sebastian played with the collar and tightened it over my body. His hand grazed my chest as he straightened out the fabric.

"Come on out into the middle of the store where I can see you in a better light." He waved his hand as my chest tightened at the thought of my body on display under all of those florescent lights.

Not that I was ashamed about my body, I put in many hours in the gym, but I've never worn a revealing shirt like this, and I was in a busy mall.

He circled around me inspecting every angle of my torso. He even put his strong hand on my shoulder and spun me around.

The storefront had floor-to-ceiling windows and customers turned their heads as they paraded by to see me in this revealing shirt. It was a thrill being an exhibit like that.

"You have to take this shirt. You just look too sexy in it to pass it up." He licked his lips.

"I have to agree with you, but it's eighty bucks."

"New position, new wardrobe, remember?" he said. "Now how about some new jeans?"

I shook my head no, although I knew I needed at least one pair without holes in the crotch. I didn't want to blow my first paycheck before I'd even gotten it.

Before I knew it, he put a pair in my hands. They were a fine pair of jeans. The denim was smooth and elastic with a slight bit of a shimmer.

The stitching on the pockets alone were enough to make me weep. But $200? "Maybe another day," I said.

"Your loss." He rolled his eyes and took them back from me. "Let me ring that shirt up for you."

I headed back to the fitting room to change into my original clothes. Before I did so, I noticed myself in the mirror again. Damn, I loved that shirt.

I rubbed my hands over my chest and abs, which appeared even more defined through the shirt. They should make underwear out of this fabric.

My cock engorged, and I grabbed it over my shorts. The sexual tension was unbearable.

Sebastian talked with some female customers, giving them number cards and directing them to fitting rooms. He was just five feet away, separated from my hungry monster by only one thin fitting room door.

We'd scanned each other like hungry animals in our torso-flattering see-through shirts. I wanted him now.

I undid the zipper on my shorts and grabbed my dick, I pulled it out from under my underwear and rubbed it against the smooth fabric of the mesh shirt.

It felt so sensual that I couldn't stop rubbing myself. I took the shirt off and wrapped my pole in its fabric and rubbed up and down.

Thoughts of those juicy lips surrounding my cock was tantalizing. I rotated my hips in circles as if he were on his knees in front of me and I were fucking his mouth.

The excitement of knowing he was out there was all too much. A cloud of pleasure overcame me and I shot my load onto the floor underneath the bench. I didn't want to get my shirt dirty before even paying for it.

When it hit me that I'd just pleasured myself in a public place, I panicked, rubbed the semen into the carpet with my shoe, threw on my old shirt, and stuffed my deflating erection back into my pants and hurried out.

"You sure took a long time getting dressed." He had a grin from ear to ear. "Next time you require assistance, feel free to ask for me," he said, making air quotes with his fingers on the word *assistance*.

I felt a little embarrassed and gave a nervous laugh before we walked to the register.

When he gave me my credit card back, his fingers skimmed over mine and my body shuddered. He placed the receipt in the bag and handed me his business card.

"Feel free to call me for all of your wardrobe needs. I like to think I give the finest customer service."

That night in bed, I couldn't stop thinking about Sebastian. I took out his business card and wiped it all over my genitals.

Thinking about how fucking hot it was to touch myself in the fitting room just feet away from where he was standing made me come twice that night. I knew I'd to go back to that store.

CHAPTER 2

THE NEXT DAY WAS A SATURDAY, and I went back to the mall hoping he would be there. I was in luck, he was, and this time there was another store employee.

The store was empty this time as well, and he was nose deep in that biology book. His wide grin showcased his dimples when he looked up at me. The female employee next to him with the name tag that said, "Angela" nodded to me.

"I should study for tomorrow's exam, but I just can't get into it." He rolled his eyes at the book. "Did you come back for those jeans I know you wanted to buy yesterday?"

"I wasn't sure if you'd be here again."

Angela leaned in to whisper to Sebastian, "Is that the guy you were talking about?"

Sebastian ignored her. "I'm always here. I practically live here." He laughed. "When I'm not in class or at swim practice, that is." He set the book down. "What prevented you from buying the jeans yesterday?"

"I've never paid $200 for a pair of jeans."

"You've earned it, with the promotion and all. Treat yourself. Dress like the successful stud that you are. Hold on, let me get them for you."

Sebastian came back with five pairs of jeans.

"How did you know my size?"

"I paid attention to you yesterday. I know my sizes and fabrics." He handed me the pair I lusted after the day before and I held them in my hands like a pirate who just discovered a gold booty.

He put his hand on the small of my back. "Come on. Let's go try those on." There was no secret that he wanted me.

This time, the shorts I wore to the store were a little bit more modern, but still not up to the standards of the store.

I undid the button and zipper and let them fall to my knees, remembering how fun it was to have my pants down in this same fitting room the day before.

There could have been angels ringing church bells when I put the jeans on. They fit perfectly and made me look trendy. In the mirror, my butt appeared firmer than I remembered. All those squats paid off.

"Are you being shy again?" Sebastian called from behind the fitting room door. "Come on out and show me the goods."

I stepped out and let Sebastian look me up and down once again, his eyes penetrating my skin.

"You look scrumptious in those jeans, but I think you might like some of the other ones I brought even better."

I raised my eyebrows at Sebastian, excited at the prospect of playing dress-up with this hot guy, but wondered if he would persuade me to spend more than I could afford.

I stepped into jeans like I was stepping into my new, enchanted life — a new me. These jeans were a far cry from anything I'd ever tried on before. $250. Ouch!

But damn, my butt looked awesome, even more-so than the last pair. My crotch had that extra oomph.

I wondered if he was still outside the door, waiting for me to come out and model, so I popped the door open a little bit to see.

Sebastian was standing there with a smug look on his face. He waved his hand for me to come all the way out.

"Those jeans make your bulge pop like it'll hit me in the face."

My stomach fluttered as energy shot down to my crotch.

"And damn do you have a nice ass." Sebastian patted my behind, and the connection was electrifying.

He didn't take his eyes off of my crotch for a second. I could feel the blood engorging me.

"I'll take them then. You seem to know what you're doing when it comes to fashion."

"Gotta check them in the better light, like we did with the shirt yesterday."

We went up to the front register. There were at least six other customers in the store now and we were in full view of them and the outside passersby. But that didn't deter Sebastian from checking me over in front of everybody.

He grabbed my ass making *humph* sounds and spun me around in front of him. He got down on his knees in the middle of the store and adjusted the jeans on my body, tugging on the hem and adjusting my crotch.

Two female customers turned around and giggled as they watched Sebastian fuss over my jeans, his head so close to my bulge. He didn't give two fucks.

"Please tell me you're going to take these," he said.

I couldn't say no, not just because I love the jeans, but because he was kneeling with his face to my growing crotch.

He continued to adjust the button fly, in full view of the windows and I kept getting harder. The outline of my trouser snake slithered down the leg.

"Ah-hem," said another woman, waiting at the counter with a sarcastic-looking grin on her face. "If I could interrupt you two gentlemen, I'd like to pay for my clothes."

She seemed more amused than angry, but the interruption brought us back to Earth.

"Vince, right?" he asked. "Let me ring these up before we both get in trouble." Sebastian rung the woman up first.

Just as I was about to walk out of the store, he stopped me. "You're not from around here, are you?"

"Minnesota. Just moved here for the job last week. Can't wait to enjoy the beach."

"And you have swimming trunks?"

"Yeah, I have board trunks I use in the pool."

He shook his head no. "That won't do. You're in Miami now. You need a Speedo."

I gulped. "I've never... I couldn't possibly wear one of those."

"Let me guide you. I'm on the swim team at the University of Miami and know a thing or two about Speedos." He stared at my crotch. "I know exactly which ones would fit you. And now that you're not quite so excited, you can try them out."

I had a serious case of blue balls by now.

He went over to the swimsuit rack on the wall near the fitting rooms. "This is a bikini cut Speedo with a low rise and a contoured pouch. It will hoist you up and give you a supportive lift.

I didn't know what the hell all that meant, but there sure wasn't a lot of fabric to that thing. And the white was almost as transparent as the shirt I bought the day before. At least I wouldn't have visible tan lines.

I think he could sense my nervousness. "It takes a while to get used to them. Just hold yourself with confidence and be proud of your hot body."

He cleared his throat. "Since you're well-endowed, keep your cock straight down over your balls to keep them snug in place." He analyzed my crotch again. "It might seem like you're protruding out in front of the world, but if you place it up or to the side, it will be even more obvious when you get excited."

He raised his eyebrows. "You're supposed to wear underwear when trying swimsuits on in the store, but I'm willing to look the other way just to see how good you look in them."

I closed the door and dropped my pants. This time, everything came off. I stood in front of the mirror naked, admiring my own body, and then pulled up the suit which stretched over my dick and left nothing to the imagination.

My cock was a little hard, but it wasn't too obvious yet. It felt good, like I wasn't wearing anything at all. I felt self-assured in the mirror, standing tall, even looking taller.

My junk needed a little adjusting before opening the door, knowing he'd be outside the door waiting to see me in the Speedo. I was happy to oblige.

"Nice!" said Sebastian. "You look fucking hot." He pulled me out of the fitting room into the middle of the store to parade me around. I knew this was coming.

The eyes of the other customers lingered over my body. At the beach, this might be normal, but I was the only one half-naked. Instead of panicking, my cock became semi-erect from all the attention.

My package protruded from the fabric. Outside the store, customers slowed down to leer at me through the window. My heart leaped out of my chest. I was simultaneously embarrassed and aroused.

"Don't you think this shows all little...too much of my package?"

"Not enough," he joked. He spun me around to face the window where a small crowd of people gathered to look me over, men and women. Some of them took pictures.

Just like he did with the jeans, Sebastian kneeled in front of me to adjust the fabric, then my package. He ran his fingers around the legs to smooth the fabric and his finger slipped under, caressing my cock.

As it grew, my erection shifted to the side. With pronounced movements, he reached into the top of the Speedos and grabbed my penis to adjust it some more and tucked it over my balls.

He stood up and toward the crowd and waved his arms to my body as if he were speaking to them. "Looks better, right?"

The crowd enjoyed the show, as did I, but they lost interest and dissipated. When the coast was clear, Sebastian made his move.

"You can't get too worked up in these, otherwise it will pop out like this." He reached in and pulled my penis so it pointed up and just the tip was above the top of the Speedo. It was hard as a rock now.

He squeezed the head twice before continuing, "This fabric wicks away sweat and dries quickly in the sun. Its form-fitting, stylish, and will last you years to come."

I couldn't believe he was giving me a sales pitch while holding onto my dick in the middle of the store with other people passing by. Angela gasped for air.

"You two need to get a room, literally. Go into the fitting room before we both get fired." Sebastian's head jerked back and eyes widened at her statement.

"Yes, I'll watch the store," she said, "if that's what you're worried about. You won't be the first one to get action in the fitting room." She winked at both Sebastian and me.

"Guess I'm on break!" Sebastian said.

He grabbed my hand and guided me to the room while I bit my lip and enjoyed heightened senses. The short walk to the fitting room seemed like it took forever.

"Don't move, Vince," was the first thing Sebastian said to me when we got into the fitting room. He leaned back to look me over. "I want to remember you like this." His words gave me goosebumps.

Like a bat out of hell, he was on his knees pushing his face right into my crotch, licking the shaft over the fabric of the Speedo, starting at the base and going down to the head as it stretched the fabric taut.

The fabric rubbing against me was a sensation I'd never felt before. Undoing the drawstring, he freed my cock from its shackles and it sprung out.

He held his breath for a moment and then his warm mouth surrounded my cock as I moaned in pleasure. He made a production when he revealed inch by inch as he pulled down the trunks.

My hard-on pulsated in his mouth. Sucking and slurping noises were loud as we could let our guard down until we heard the doorbell ring again. The store was to close in a half hour, anyway.

My meat twitched under his control and my skin prickled. He was starving for me and only I could satisfy his hunger.

His head tilted so he could take more of me down his throat. I spasmed as if jolted by electricity. He grabbed my ass which was contracting and releasing in thrusts over and over again.

Bit by bit, he slid inch by mind-blowing inch until he reached the base. My balls slapped back and forth on his chin.

Euphoria fogged my mind as I thought I would explode right there. But then he stopped and put his finger to his mouth to silence me.

A customer discussed a dress she was trying on with Angela, asking her opinion. Their voices were too muffled for me to make out their exact words, but I got the gist.

Angela chatted about this year's summer trends knowing I was naked in front of Sebastian just a few feet away. When we heard diminishing footsteps, we picked up again.

There were two knocks on the door and we froze in place. "I think you boys are missing something," Angela said.

Sebastian cracked the door and took a small plastic bag from her. "Thought you might need this," she said. Sebastian took out a condom and lube from. "Safety first," she said in a goofy voice.

"Thanks," Sebastian said.

Just as he started to close the door, she stuck her hand in and opened it back up. "Not yet." She perused me, naked in all my glory, flag full-staff and covered in Sebastian's spit.

"Too bad you're gay." She shrugged her shoulders and walked away nonchalantly. It turned me on to think about how many people had seen me naked, or at least half-naked, that day.

Sebastian stood up and kissed with me. His tongue was like a panther attacking its prey. He ripped off his shirt and undid the button on his pants.

His abs were even tighter than mine, probably from all the swimming he did. He opened the condom and put it in his mouth, holding it by his teeth between his pursed lips.

Then he got on his knees and unraveled it over my pole down to the base using only his mouth. He lowered his pants to reveal purple Andrew Christians then slung them to floor, exposing his mouth-watering ass.

Sebastian leaned me up against the wall of the fitting room and lubed himself up before leaning backwards into my body and onto my cock.

Squeaks and moans of pleasure escaped his fleshy lips as I thrust myself into him, rocking the fitting rooms. Just as I was about to blow, he pulled away. His ass made a distinctive *pop* as my dick fell out.

"I changed my mind. I want to taste you." He flung the condom off and took control of my manhood with one hand and barely kissed the head with his lips.

He sat there, mouth open, waiting for me to expel into him. I plunged my hips in and around his mouth. The orgasm was sudden, and I lost my breath before exploding.

With each spurt, my body shook. He swallowed me down his greedy throat. His luscious lips swept over my shaft as he pulled back.

There were a few more jolts of cum that oozed onto his face and neck. He licked his lips and gulped the rest down his warm throat. I was exhausted. Deflated.

As I dressed, Sebastian snatched the underwear out of my hands.

"What's that for?"

"I'll let you take the Speedos for free if you let me keep your underwear as a souvenir. I'm a little kinky that way."

He put them up to his face and took a big whiff. They were still damp from sweating in the heat.

I couldn't believe someone would want to keep my underwear, that was so...strange...and hot. He wanted to smell me even after I left.

"Sure, it's a deal," I said.

"We like to take good care of our customers."

"Won't you get in trouble for missing merchandise?" I asked as we walked out of the fitting rooms and toward the front register.

He thought about it. "If they suspect anything is missing, I guess they'll look through the security cameras."

My heart sank do the floor. I didn't want to get arrested.

"Oh man, the security camera *definitely* saw everything." Angela could barely contain her laughter. "I'd delete it, but nah, it's *my* souvenir."

My blood ran could and all I could respond with was a whimper. "But don't worry," she said. "If the security guard finds the tape, I'll blow him to keep him quiet."

"Welcome to Miami," Sebastian said.

ABOUT THE AUTHOR

Hi, I'm Nico. I love to write gay stories about public sex, cruising, bathhouses, anything taboo and a little bit dirty.

When I'm not writing, I love hanging out at the bars and binge-watching Netflix alike.

If you enjoyed this book, sign up for the Mailing List and receive a FREE book.

See you next time

-Nico

Join the Mailing List

For more information:
www.NicoFoxAuthor.com

ALSO BY NICO FOX

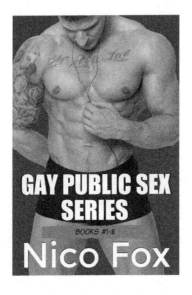

The complete Gay Public Sex Series box set. **Eight** steamy M/M erotic stories full of **public** encounters.

This bundle includes:

Bulge on a Train

Truck Stop Fantasy

Fitting Room Temptation

Ferris Wheel Threesome

Hole in the Wall Exhibitionist

Ride-Share Stripper

Gay Resort Weekend

Art Gallery Awakening

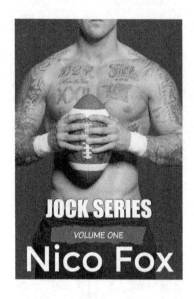

The first Jock Series box set. **Six** steamy M/M erotic stories full of **sweaty athletic guys**.

This bundle includes:

Captain of the Swim Team

First Time, First Down

Soccer Jockstrap

Slammed By the Team

Team Catcher

Heavyweight Punch

The first DILF Series box set. Six stories about
hot daddies and their younger counterparts.

This bundle includes:

DILF of My Dreams

Seduced by the DILF

My Boss is a DILF

First Time Gay with My Girlfriend's Dad

My Girlfriend's Dad Wants It

First Time Gay with the DILF Professor

"I always follow his lead about anything and everything. All of our friends do. He uses his charm and imposing stature to convince us to do anything he wants."

Finn always had a crush on his best friend, Cameron, who is *very* popular with the girls. Standing next to well-built, captain of the football team, and all-around stud Cameron makes Finn feel a little, shall we say, less than…insecure.

Cameron has always protected Finn from others when they make fun of him for his small stature and he's always felt secure with him.

Finn invites Cameron over for a night of video games and beer only to be shocked when Cameron makes a wager on a game that Finn can't say no to. Who says fantasies don't come true?

Dustin has landed his dream job in Silicon Valley just one month
after graduating college. He tries to keep his head down as much
as he can, despite being surrounded by **hyper-masculine
alphas** that call each other ***bro.*** He just can't stop lusting after
the company's founder, notorious womanizer and billionaire's
son, Brett.

The company is in peril. A bug in their software may cause one
of their biggest customers to leave them. Everyone in the office is
nervous, but they try to cover it up with heavy drinking after
work and carrying on with their secret Santa ritual.

But Dustin solves the bug, making him the company hero. Brett
is eternally grateful to his new employee for saving his company.
Find out how this straight stud will pay back his employee in this
new erotic story from Nico Fox.

Angels and Devils

Nico Fox

A SEXY underground Halloween party...

"It's amazing how far two people in love will go to hide their inner desires from each other."

Lucas is a shy college student. His boyfriend, Colton, is an extroverted sports stud that every guy on campus wants to get with. Together, they have the perfect relationship. Or so it seems.

Lucas is worried someone will steal Colton away because he's such a catch. What's more, Lucas doesn't know if he can trust himself to handle monogamy.

They head into Manhattan to look for the perfect Halloween costumes for their upcoming school party. They want sexy costumes to show off all that hard work in the gym.

At the costume store, they meet Ace, a sophisticated New Yorker throwing his own Halloween party, one where inhibitions are thrown to the wind.

Ace seems a little shady. The party is so elusive that they need to be blindfolded as they ride in a limo to the party. But that's the price Lucas is willing to pay to go to a real New York City party.

How will Lucas and Colton's relationship hold up after a wild night at the party? Will jealousy get in the way, or will exploration bring their relationship to new heights?

Printed in Great Britain
by Amazon

Eyes lingered over my body

Vince just got a sweet promotion and
needs a sweet new wardrobe to dress the
part. He heads to a fancy Miami Beach
mall and meets Sebastian, a hot, sexy
store employee who helps him pick out a
trendy new shirt, one that Vince would
never have picked out for himself.

The sexual tension between the two is
immediate. Sebastian's attention and
subtle flirtations get Vince all worked up
that he just can't help himself when he
gets back to the fitting room.

Vince goes back to the store but, this time,
a little more confident and ready to step
up his game, but unaware of what's in
store for him and Sebastian as the day
goes on. He'll be pleasantly surprised
when Sebastian suggests he try wearing a
Speedo in the store.

Learn more about Nico:
nicofoxauthor.com
amazon.com/author/nicofox
twitter.com/nicofoxauthor
facebook.com/nicofoxauthor

ISBN 9798669801588

9 798669 801588

90000